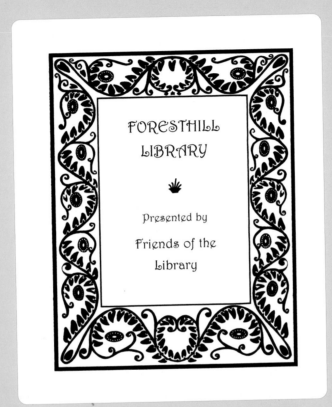

Kit & Kaboodle

ROSEMARY WELLS

GODWINBOOKS

HENRY HOLT AND COMPANY • NEW YORK

These are the stories of KIT and KABOODLE,
who were very good . . .

 and Spinka, who wasn't.

Sock Mischief

Kit and Kaboodle never made any trouble.

So why did a mischief-making mouse wearing
a little red hat come to their house?

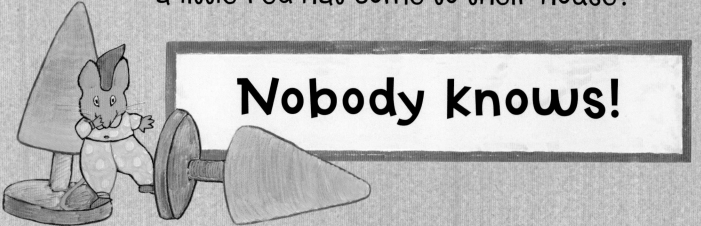

Nobody knows!

Granny made shamrock socks for Kaboodle and daffodil socks for Kit.

They wore them everywhere.

But Spinka was not happy about the socks.

The reason was that Granny had not made
a pair of socks for Spinka's feet.

The socks got very dirty.

Mama tossed them into the washing machine.

She turned the knob
to **COLD** water
so the socks
wouldn't shrink.

Kit and Kaboodle
waited and **waited**
for their socks to
come out of the wash.

Spinka watched
the twins drift
off to sleep.

Then Spinka turned the knob from **COLD** to **HOT**.

When the wash was done, she pushed the door open and dropped a fishing line into the machine.

First she caught a daffodil sock, then a shamrock sock.

Next she popped them into the dryer and pushed the **HOT** air button.

Kit and Kaboodle and Mama and Daddy
looked high and low for the missing socks.

None turned up.

Kit and Kaboodle had to ask Granny
to make new socks.

The missing socks never reappeared.
And the reason was . . .

the socks
fit Spinka
perfectly!

Saturday was baseball day. Daddy dropped a box of brand-new, snow-white baseballs in his duffle. Kit packed his cleats and his bat. Kaboodle packed his glove and his hat.

"Ready, ready, ready to rock and roll!" said Daddy.

Spinka was **mad, mad, mad!**

The reason was that she was not invited to the baseball game.

Kit, Kaboodle, and Daddy zipped down the
elevator and sped to Central Park
on the subway.

It was a perfect day for baseball in the park.

But the baseballs were **nowhere** to be found!

So they had to play with one dirty practice ball.

When Mr. Bobbleton hit a
home run into the lake, the ball
sank, and the game was over.

Everybody
went home.

They went to eat their blimpies.
Mama said, "Oh no! I made four beautiful chocolate
blimpies. Now there are only three!"

Who knew where the fourth blimpie went?

It was bath time.
"Mama, where is your birthday bubble bath
from Paris?" asked Kaboodle.
"It's so pink and it smells so good!" said Kit.
"Just one drop each," said Mama.

Kaboodle ran the water.
Kit squeezed out two drops
of Foame de France.

Someone was
hiding behind the
toothbrushes.

"I want the valentine pajamas!" said Kit.
"I got them first," said Kaboodle.
"It's spaceship-pajama night!" said Mama.

While no one was looking, the Foame de France
foamed up the whole bathroom.

"Kit!" said Mama. "Kaboodle! You used up all my bubble bath!"

Spinka laughed her twinkly laugh, but no one could hear her and no one could see her behind the toothbrushes.

Daddy read their story. Mama sang their good-night song.
Suddenly they heard a faint buzzing noise.

"Someone left the toothbrush on!" said Mama.
But it wasn't Kit. And it wasn't Kaboodle.

It was Spinka with the electric toothbrush!

Teeth clean, Spinka fell asleep making plans for tomorrow. Not for big tubs of trouble . . .

just a teaspoon of trouble!

For Kathie Sawyer,

with thanks to Johanna Hurley

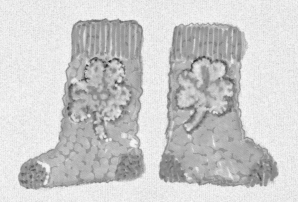

Henry Holt and Company, *Publishers since 1866*

Henry Holt® is a registered trademark of Macmillan Publishing Group, LLC

175 Fifth Avenue, New York, New York 10010 • mackids.com

Library of Congress Cataloging-in-Publication Data is available.

ISBN 978-1-250-13075-4

Our books may be purchased in bulk for promotional, educational, or business use.

Please contact your local bookseller or the Macmillan Corporate and Premium Sales Department

at (800) 221-7945 ext. 5442 or by e-mail at MacmillanSpecialMarkets@macmillan.com.

First edition, 2018 / Design by April Ward

Printed in China by RR Donnelley Asia Printing Solutions Ltd., Dongguan City, Guangdong Province

1 3 5 7 9 10 8 6 4 2